Get On My Bus

Written by Andy Donnell
&
Illustrated by Mike Phillips

Dedicated to my Dad, who taught me the importance of treating others with respect and to always believe in myself.
– Andy Donnell –

Published in 2018 by A Spark in the Sand
Edited by Emma Pullar

94 Beach St
Askam-in-Furness
Cumbria
LA16 7BH
England

www.asparkinthesand.co.uk

ISBN 978-1-9998240-7-5

This book belongs to

Let's hit the road!

Liam the leprechaun sat in his garden, feeling very sad. His house was falling down, his garden was a jungle and he had nothing to eat except a stale loaf of bread.

"If only I could find some work," he sighed.

The leprechaun was a builder who'd moved over from Ireland many years ago. There was lots of work in England then, building roads and houses everywhere, no need to hunt for treasure like his grandfather did. But those days were long gone and Liam was tired of being poor. But he was not one who gave up easily.

Brushing the dirt off his shabby clothes and picking up his knobbly walking stick, he marched into town as he'd done every day for years. He was always hopeful of finding a job, but he never did. All he found was other little people like himself desperate for money to buy the things they needed. Some folks had tried to magic their problems away but magic can't solve all your problems, though Liam sometimes wished it could.

"What am I going to do?" he muttered to himself.

As Liam returned home, the air grew chilly. Looking up, he saw a big black cloud drifting towards the sun. It started to rain and as if by magic, a huge rainbow appeared in the sky. Liam stared at it in wonder.

"That's so beautiful," he whispered.

The cloud passed and the rainbow disappeared as fast as it had arrived. But the colours stayed in his mind, making him feel strange. It was as if the rainbow was trying to tell him something, but he didn't know what. He puzzled for ages until it hit him...

"The pot of gold!" he gasped.

Legends say there is a pot of gold at the end of every rainbow and anyone who finds it can keep it.

"That's what I must do!" Liam cried eagerly. "I must travel to where that rainbow ended and claim the gold. Then all my money worries – and those of my friends – will be over!"

Feeling giddy with excitement, Liam the leprechaun raced across to his barn. Pulling open the creaking wooden door, he stepped inside and gasped with horror. The bus in which he used to drive everyone to work was in a worse state than his house.

"This'll never get me to rainbow's end," he groaned.

There was a knock at the door. It was Liam's neighbour, a hard-working little sprite, called Chas.

Liam told Chas all about his plan to find the pot of gold. "Except I don't think I'll get there on this old heap," he added.

"Course you will!" Chas cried, slapping him on the back. "I'm an engineer, remember. I'll help you fix it...if I can come with you."

"Deal!" laughed Liam.

The bus hadn't been used for years and was covered in dirt and cobwebs.

"Mind you don't get caught in one of those, Chas," chuckled Liam.

"I may be small, but I'm not a fly!" she laughed back.

After many buckets of hot soapy water and a good hosing down, the old bus gleamed almost like new.

Time for the moment of truth, would the bus work or was it too badly broken? Chas got busy with her spanner while Liam waited to start the engine.

"Try it now," she called, bending down behind the bus.

VROOOM, VROOOM! The engine fired, the exhaust sending dusty black clouds all over Chas.

"TURN IT OFF!" she yelled, coughing and spluttering. When the smoke cleared, her face was black with soot!

After a quick wash in one of the buckets, Chas was ready to go.

"The end of the rainbow was just behind that hill over there," said Liam. "We should be there and back in a couple of hours."

He jumped up behind the wheel and Chas sat on one of the seats.

"Just imagine," she said, her eyes day-dreamy, "by the end of today we'll have enough money to buy some food and proper clothes."

"That's why I really want to get going," said Liam, starting the engine again. "We must make sure we get there first. The elves have a lot of money and if they find out what we're up to, they might try to find the pot of gold and keep it for themselves."

"Wait for me!" called a voice.

Brendan was hurrying towards them, waving madly. He was another leprechaun and good friends with them both.

"Wherever you're going, I want to come too!" he puffed.

When Chas and Liam told him their mission, Brendan was even more excited than they were.

"Come on! What are we waiting for?" he cried, jumping onto the back of the bus. "Let's hit the road!"

Jerking and grinding because it hadn't been used for so long, the bus set off towards the hill in the distance.

"Let's sing a song!" cried Liam.

"I've thought of a great song for a trip like this," cheered Brendan.

"You start and we'll follow." Chas beamed, holding her arms up like the conductor of an orchestra. "Ready? One, two, three..."

'Up and down we go, bouncing to-and-fro,

Bumpy bumpy little bus, lots of room for all of us,

Over the hills and far away,

We'll find the pot of gold today!'

Driving on, they soon reached the hill and the old bus ground slowly up the steep slope.

"Can't wait to get to the other side!" cried Brendan, saying what they were all thinking.

They drove over top and down the other side, expecting to see the pot of gold sparkling in the sunshine. But there was nothing. It wasn't there!

The three friends were so upset, they didn't notice the dark clouds gathering above. The rain began with big drops that splashed all around them but soon became a downpour, drenching the little magic folk.

"Have you got raincoats in the bus?" yelled Chas.

"No, I didn't bring any!" said Liam.

"What about a big umbrella?" Brendan asked.

"Didn't bring one of those either," said Liam.

"We're getting soaked!" sighed Chas.

"I could use a bit of leprechaun magic?" said Brendan.

"No!" Liam held his hand up to stop his friend, "Magic and wishes don't solve problems, we can figure this out."

The rain poured down in torrents and the only place to shelter was a small tree with a few thin branches and leaves above. The friends huddled together, cold and miserable, as their clothes became soaked and water ran down their necks. Nobody spoke. They sat in silence waiting for the storm to pass. When it did, the sun came out again and it was hotter than before.

"I know a great way to get dry!" laughed Chas, holding her arms out and dancing around in the sunshine. Soon everyone's clothes were warm and dry.

"Maybe we should turn back, that storm was pretty scary!" Liam said.

"No fear!" said Brendan. "We want to stay with you and find that pot of gold."

Feeling happy again, Liam drove the bus on down the road with Brendan and Chas keeping look-out at the back for any signs of the pot of gold left behind by the rainbow. They spent the rest of the morning searching in vain and stopped the bus at lunchtime for a break.

"I'm sooooooo hungry," said Brendan, holding his rumbling stomach. "Don't suppose you've got any food in the bus?"

"No, sorry," replied Liam. "Never occurred to me to pack any."

"But we've got to have something to eat..."

"It's okay, Brendan," Chas interrupted him. "I know just what to do."

She rubbed her hands together and began chanting a spell.

"No, Chas!" Liam stepped in front of her, "We don't need magic, look!"

Liam pointed to a nearby orchard. The trees were heavy with apples.

"We can't eat those, Liam," Brendan said. "They're much too high for us to pick. We're only small and you won't let us use magic."

"More importantly, the apples belong to the farmer who owns the trees. It would be stealing to take them," said Chas.

"We can take the windfalls," Brendan cried, running towards some apples lying on the ground. The fallen apples were sure to rot soon and would be wasted. The three friends collected as many apples as they could carry and took them back to the bus where they ate their fill and kept the rest for later.

"All aboard! Off we go again!" Liam said.

The friends sang their traveling song all afternoon long.

'Up and down we go, bouncing to-and-fro,
Bumpy bumpy little bus, lots of room for all of us,
Over the hills and far away,
We'll find the pot of gold today!'

"We've got a flat tyre," cried Liam, jumping down from the driver's seat as the bus bumped to a stop.

"I'll get the spare wheel from the back," said Chas.

"Don't forget the jack to lift the bus up so we can change the wheel," Brendan called.

Chas returned with the spare wheel, but no jack.

"Didn't you check there was one?" she asked Liam.

"No, I was in too much of a hurry to get going," he replied.

"Then we're really stuck now," sighed Chas.

Everyone looked at each other, wondering what to do next

"Okay, I think it's time for a little magic, what can it hurt?" Liam said.

Brendan and Chas shrugged.

Liam held tight to his knobbly walking stick, lifted it in the air and slammed it down into the ground.

"Broken bus, lift up for us!"

He raised his walking stick and the bus started to rise.

"It's working!" Chas clapped her hands.

There was a puff of glitter and Liam's stick began to shake.

"Oh no!" He cried.

The bus crashed to the ground.

"You were right, Liam." Brendan sighed, "Magic doesn't solve problems."

It was then that Brendan spotted a length of wood lying in a ditch. It looked thick and strong.

"Come on, Liam," he urged. "We can use this to lift the bus."

It was hard work pulling the plank out of the ditch and even harder work to make it raise the bus. But they managed it by standing together on one end and jumping up and down on the wood. This gave Chas just enough time to slip the old wheel off and put the new one on. Once again, they were able to continue on their journey.

"We make a great team," said Liam, as they drove off towards the setting sun.

As night fell, the three friends felt sad that they had still not found the post of gold Liam stopped the bus.

"What do we do now?" asked Chas.

The other two didn't know what she meant.

"We haven't got a tent or sleeping bags or even an old blanket to keep warm?"

Liam was embarrassed.

"I didn't think—"

"Yes, we know," Brendan cut in. "Nobody did any planning for this trip and magic is not the answer."

There was no choice but to spend the night out in the open. But it was no fun sleeping under the stars. The ground was hard, the moon was too bright and it was cold — really cold! They sat together beside the bus, yawning and shivering, all wishing they were back home in their warm beds. As the night wore on, they managed to drop off to sleep and woke up next morning stiff and aching in every limb. Without speaking, they ate the last of the apples, drank some water from a stream and set off again on their quest.

The friends were now quite far from home and none of them recognised the countryside. It wasn't long before they were completely lost.

"Have you got a map?" Chas asked Liam.

"Yes I have," he answered, reaching into the pocket of the driver's door. But the map had got wet and was a soggy mess. This was the last straw! They started to quarrel.

"Why didn't you think about these things before we started?" Brendan shouted.

"I told you, I was in a hurry!" said Liam.

"That's no excuse!" snorted Chas.

"How come it's all down to me?" Liam protested. "You two didn't think of anything either!"

And so it went on, arguing and blaming, until they all burst into tears.

"STOP!" Liam shouted. "Everyone stop arguing, right now!"

Chas and Brendan looked at him in surprise.

"We've known each other for long time." Liam continued. "We're good friends — 'besties' as the human children say..."

"Besties?" Brendan said surprised. "They don't call each other chummy wummy? How silly!"

Chas rolled her eyes.

"I think what Liam is trying to say," she smiled at Liam, "Is that we shouldn't be quarrelling. We should be working together to solve our problems like we did yesterday. We can't be a great team if we're fighting with each other."

The other two nodded in agreement. Then Chas held out her arms and they had a group hug. "Let's go home," suggested Liam.

"You mean, give up the quest for the gold?" Brendan gasped.

"Not at all!" said Liam.

"I mean, let's start over. We should have planned this trip better."

Liam turned the bus around but as they drove on, the friends became worried. Nothing looked familiar. They stopped at a crossroads and there were several different roads they could choose.

"Let's try them one by one," suggested Brendan.

"We don't have enough fuel left to do that," Liam said. "The gauge is very low already."

"I could do a guiding spell." Brendan offered. Liam shook his head.

"What do you reckon then, Chas?" asked Brendan, turning round. There was no answer... and no sign of their companion!

Chas was running towards a signpost she had spotted, but when she got there she found it was broken. The sign that showed the way back to town pointed down at the ground.

"Doesn't matter," she called to the boys, climbing up the post like a monkey. "I can see the right way from up here."

The other roads led to farmyards and cowsheds, but one big one snaked away into the distance.

"This way!" she shouted.

Liam drove the old bus down the long twisty road and, at last, his cottage appeared on the horizon. They were nearly there when the engine coughed a few times and then died.

"Run out of fuel," he sighed.

There was nothing else for it but to push the bus the last bit of the way. Being the lightest, Chas jumped into the driver's seat and the two leprechauns took their places at the back. They heaved and strained, just managing to get the heavy vehicle moving and keep it rolling down the road.

"Almost there!" Chas called from the front.

"Thank goodness for that," puffed Brendan, wiping the sweat out of his eyes with the back of his hand. "Can't do this for much longer."

They rolled the old bus into Liam's yard and when it stopped, Chas jumped down and hurried into the house.

"I'll make us all a nice cup of tea," she called.

"Then we must talk about our second trip," said Brendan.

The tea made everyone feel better and it was exciting to discuss another journey soon.

"If we learn from our mistakes, we might have a real shot at finding the gold this time," said Brendan excitedly.

"That's right," Liam agreed. "We must plan carefully before we go next time and make sure we take everything with us that we're likely to need."

"The good thing about all the mistakes we made on this trip is that it's brought us all closer together," added Chas.

"Yes, and now we'll be unstoppable!" said Liam.

"Here's to an unstoppable team!" Brendan raised his cup of tea triumphantly and toppled backwards off his chair, slashing tea over his beard. He blinked and spluttered, half empty teacup still in his hand.

The three friends laughed and laughed.

All About Teamwork

A few days later, Chas and Brendan were back at Liam's house helping to get everything ready for their second attempt to find the pot of gold.

"Got the tent, Liam?" Brendan called.

"I've already loaded it onto the bus," he replied.

"And I'm just putting my toolbox in now," added Chas.

"What about the map?" asked Liam.

"I've got it here,," Brendan replied. "I think we should go south this time. We were looking in the wrong place over to the west."

By mid-morning everything was packed and they were ready to go. Liam jumped into the driver's seat and Chas made herself comfy behind him. But Brendan hung back, standing apart and looking thoughtful.

"What's the problem?" called Chas.

"We could use all the help we can get," he told his friends. "We've got all the stuff we need, but I think we could do with a few more helpers."

The three friends set off along Leprechaun Lane towards a cottage with a little pond in front of it. Liam had had the clever idea of asking two gnomes for help.

"Albert is the cleverest gnome I've ever met," explained Liam. "There isn't anything he can't do."

"Give us an example," said Brendan.

"There's so many," Liam said enthusiastically. "He can make things, mend things, knows where to find things,, solve problems — all sorts of stuff like that. Best of all, though, he's a brilliant map-reader. Many years ago he led an expedition that discovered Crooked-Stick Mountain."

"We definitely need Albert's help, none of us are as clever as that," chuckled Chas. "Who's the other gnome?"

"His wife, Violet," Liam said. "She's intuitive, they say she has the wisdom of an ancient dragon, and I'm told her cooking is talked about all over the Land."

"Cooking?" said Brendan. "I can't wait to meet Violet, I'm gonna make sure she's my new chummy wummy." He patted his round tummy.

"A new chummy wummy to help you fill your podgy tummy!" Chas giggled, poking Brendan in the stomach.

"Hey!" Brendan rubbed his round tum and laughed. Liam laughed too.

"Look! There they are." He pointed to two figures waving behind a garden gate in the distance.

Chas and Brendan waited outside while Liam went indoors to speak to the gnomes. He told them all about their quest for the pot of gold.

"We'd like you to come with us," he said at the end.

"Really?" cried Albert, looking pleased. "That's wonderful. We haven't had a holiday for ages."

"It's not exactly a holiday..."

"Of course it is!" Violet said, clapping her hands together with glee. "And we could certainly do with some gold."

Liam stood up.

"So you'll come then?"

"We'd love to," said Albert, shaking Liam's hand.

"Right! I'll fetch the bus while you get your stuff ready. We'll pick you up in ten!"

When Liam, Chas and Brendan arrived, Violet was waiting with a huge sack.

"I'm looking forward to making my special dishes for you all," she chuckled, dumping the sack pots and pans onto the bus with a clatter and a clang. Albert followed her out of the house with a small suitcase and something folded up in a thin canvas bag.

"What's that?" Chas asked.

"Oh, nothing important," he answered casually.

Soon they were off and the gnomes began to sing a new song.

'With pointed hats and big bright boots,

Gnomes are the best at doing toots

We toot all day, we toot all night,

We toot and give your gran a fright!"

Chas giggled and whispered to Brendan, "I prefer our song."

Brendan nodded in agreement and then accidentally let out a loud parp! His cheeks pinked.

"That's the spirit!" Albert clapped Brendan on the back and everyone laughed.

Liam drove the merry bunch south. They spotted a fairy grove, a pink bubbling stream, but no rainbows and no pots of gold. They decided to stop for the night in a quiet spot beside the little pink river. The sun was shining, the water was sparkling and the birds were singing.

"This trip has been great so far,," Liam said to himself. "Nothing's going to go wrong this time."

Liam set about putting up the big tent in which they could all sleep while Chas cleaned the bugs off the bus. Brendan fetched some water and Albert studied the map. Violet began the very important job of preparing supper and soon the smell of purple puffs and rainbow raisins came wafting across the meadow, making everyone feel very hungry.

"Hope you like gnome cooking!" said Violet, cheerfully.

After several helpings of the tasty gnome delicacies, they all turned in for the night. Next morning they were up bright and early, keen to get on the road again.

"Not so fast," called Violet. "Breakfast first."

"What are we having? More purple puffs?" said Brendan, rubbing his hands together.

"For breakfast? Heavens!" Violet giggled.

"I like sugar stars. We used to have that at Sprite Camp when I was little," added Chas.

"You're still little!" laughed Liam.

Violet served the first of her special dishes for breakfast.

"I got up at the crack of dawn to make it," she said proudly, tipping the slop onto Brendan's plate with her ladle.

"What is it?" he asked curiously, poking the green gloop that seemed to be moving and looked suspiciously like bogies.

"It's gobblegum porridge," Violet, slopped some gloop onto Chas's plate and the sprite's nose wrinkled.

"May I have corn flakes instead?"

"Sorry. It's this or nothing!"

Chas stared with curiosity at the undulating gloop, she flinched when a blob of green sprung up onto her spoon.

"Chas! Liam!" Brendan shouted, "You gotta try this!"

Brendan's tummy had blown up like a balloon and he was floating a few feet off the ground, he continues to scrum down the gobblegum porridge.

At midday, when they stopped for lunch, Violet made some special soup.

"What's in it?" asked Liam, looking at the pot in dismay.

"It's a secret recipe," Violet winked.

"It's called jumble jelly soup. You'll never taste anything like it!"

The smell coming from the soup was not like any jelly Liam had ever eaten, it smelled more like the slime found at the bottom of a pond and old socks.

"And I never will," Liam muttered under his breath, taking his bowl away and tipping it behind a bush. But she was on him like a flash.

"You ate that so quickly! You must be hungry! Here – have seconds!" And she filled his bowl to the brim again.

Liam, Chas and Brendan snuck off while the two gnomes finished their lunch.

"I can't take much more of Violet's cooking," Chas said, her face a little green.

"I like it!" said Brendan.

"We're wasting time to keep stopping to eat," Liam whispered, "from now on we eat the sandwiches I packed. They'll be a little stale but after tasting some of the mystery food Violet serves up, I'm happy to eat two-day-old sandwiches."

The bus set off again and Liam drove the merry bunch through the lush green countryside of the south. Everyone except Violet kept a sharp look-out for the treasure.

"It's hard work cooking lovely meals all the time, I'm going to catch forty winks," she said.

About mid-morning, they rounded a corner and skidded to a halt. The road ahead crossed a wide ditch full of mud, smelly water, brambles and stinging nettles... and the bridge was down!

"What do we do now?" cried Chas.

"Can't you leprechauns and sprites do a little magic to repair the bridge?" asked Violet, who'd woken with a start when the bus pulled up sharp.

"Liam says magic can't solve problems," sighed Brendan, "and besides, none of us have enough spark to fix that bridge."

"Don't panic," said Liam. "This is just the sort of problem Albert is ace at solving."

"Look, there he goes now!" said Brendan, pointing to the gnome who had jumped down from the bus and was marching off with his canvas bag. So they sat and waited for Albert to report back, but an hour went by and he still didn't arrive.

"Where's he got to?" asked Brendan.

He glanced over at Violet, she had fallen asleep again.

"Over there!" Chas gasped. "What in sparkles is he doing?"

Albert was sitting beside a large pond. He'd taken his fishing rod out of the bag, screwed it together and was patiently waiting for a bite.

Brendan marched over to him.

"What are you doing?" he demanded.

"Fishing," replied Albert, looking puzzled at such a silly question. "That's what gnomes do."

"Why aren't you fixing the broken bridge?"

"Fixing the bridge?" Albert chucked, "Now, why would I do something like that?"

"Oh, I dunno, so we can get across, maybe?"

Albert shrugged.

"I'm retired. No more fixing stuff for me."

"What?"

"I retired last month, when I turned two hundred."

"You didn't say!"

"You didn't ask!"

"So you won't help us?"

"Nope," answered Albert, reeling his line in and casting it out again. "Other than a spot of map-reading, I'm just goin' fishin' on this holiday."

Because Albert refused to fix the bridge, there was no choice but to drive on hoping to find another way across the ditch. It took a long time and it was midday before they were back on the road again.

Albert kept his promise to read the map and the travellers found themselves at the top of steep hill overlooking the countryside below.

"We've searched high and low for the pot of gold at the end of the rainbow but without a rainbow to follow, how are we supposed to find the treasure? It could be anywhere,"," said Albert, "so I think we should try looking over by that big lake down there."

Chas side-eyed Albert.

"Are you sure that's the only reason you want us to check out the lake?"

Albert shrugged.

"I think we should try Albert's idea," said Liam, pleased that Albert was helping at last. Liam started the engine and the bus trundled down the other side of the hill to the water's edge.

As soon as Liam stopped the bus by the water's edge, Albert got out his fishing rod.

"I don't believe it!" cried Liam.

Chas pointed an accusing finger at the old gnome.

"I knew it!"

"All you want to go is go fishing!" yelled Brendan.

"Got it in one, pal!" Albert answered with a cheeky grin.

Liam, Chas and Brendan were furious. They moved away from the two gnomes so they could talk in private.

"This is ridiculous!" exclaimed Chas.

"They're not being very helpful are they?" sighed Brendan.

"Yes, but we're to blame again," Liam whispered, not wanting the gnomes to overhear their conversation. "We should have known Albert only intended to go fishing. He's two hundred years old, after all. We should have made it clear what we wanted with a mission statement."

"Bless you!" said Chas.

"I didn't sneeze, Chas, I said mission statement," laughed Liam.

"Oh, I know what that is!" Chas said, "You mean we should have told the gnomes exactly what we were aiming to do. Then Violet and Albert wouldn't have thought this trip was some sort of holiday."

"Exactly!" Liam nodded.

"Another important lesson we've learned the hard way," murmured Brendan.

It had been a grey old day then the sun came out and something in the distance gleamed as bright as a sunflower, but it wasn't a flower.

"The pot of gold!" yelled Chas.

All of a sudden two elves on motorbikes came roaring past, startling the group of friends.

The elves raced towards the treasure, knocking Liam flying. Luckily he wasn't hurt – but the keys to the bus flew out of his pocket and landed in the lake with a plop.

Whooping and shrieking in triumph, the elves made off with the gold.

Liam and his friends exchanged sad glances, then stood in stunned silence.

"It's gone! They took the entire pot of gold!" yelled Chas, she nodded towards the gnomes sat by the side of the lake. "This is all their fault! If they'd been more of a team –"

"It's not their fault!" argued Brendan. "We should have been faster. "The elves beat us to it and they're not the type to share."

"None of that matters now anyway," said Liam wearily. "We've lost the keys, we can't get home."

They went over to tell the other the bad news... and found Albert was still fishing!

"Before you say anything, you'll notice I'm not using a float," he said. "I'm dragging my hook up and down under the water."

"Why?" queried Chas.

He jerked the line into the air, there was something dangling from the end, dripping with mud and weeds.

"The keys!" cheered Liam.

The friends danced around in celebration. The gnome slapped his thighs and clapped his hands on his backside, the way gnomes do. The leprechauns did a little jig and swung each other round and round. The sprite skipped and waved her arms in the air, until she noticed Violet wasn't celebrating with them.

"Where's Violet?" Chas asked the others, "Not even she could sleep through this racket."

No sooner had Chas spoken, Violet appeared.

"I found a farm shop a little further down the bank, they didn't have much in the way of gnome cuisine, I'm afraid." Violet said, walking towards them, carrying a basket full of treats. She unpacked freshly baked loaves of bread, cheese, homemade lemonade, strawberries, cream and all sorts of other goodies. Real food, no more gnome cooking!

They spread a picnic cloth on the ground beside the lake and sat down to enjoy the feast together. Brendan was the first to start stuffing his face.

"It may not be a gold," he mumbled, chubby cheeks full of cheese, "but I feel like I've won the jackpot!"

They all giggled.

All aboard the bus, Liam started the engine and began the long drive home. Chas leaned forward and tapped Liam on the shoulder.

"What are we going to do now?" she said. "The elves will never share that pot of gold with us."

"That was a pot of gold," explained Liam, careful to keep his eyes on the road. "After the next rainbow, there'll be another pot of gold and we're going to get it!"

Liam drove the bus through the night, while the others slept. He didn't feel tired, he could sometimes stay awake for days. By the time dawn had broken, the gnome village was in sight. When they reached the little cottage, Liam, Chas and Brendan bid goodbye to the gnomes. Albert immediately started fishing in the garden pond while Violet went indoors, probably to cook up a strange breakfast. Then Liam drove home and the three weary friends sat round his picnic table again.

"What now?" asked Brendan.

"We pray for rain," said Chas.

There was no tea left in the house, so Chas brought out three glasses of water and they sat together sipping them thoughtfully.

"Brendan was right when he said we were learning the hard way," Liam said after a while. "Lesson one—"

"—was not planning the first trip properly," Chas interrupted, "and failing to take the important things we needed."

"And lesson two?" asked Liam, raising his eyebrows at Brendan.

"Um ..." Brendan's eyes looked skyward in thought, "Not explaining the plan properly to the gnomes?"

"That's right!" Liam said.

Brendan smiled at his own cleverness.

"We need to be a better team if we're going to succeed." Chas offered.

"We do," Liam agreed, "It all went wrong because Albert and Violet were doing one thing and we were doing another."

"Next time ..." Chas smiled at the leprechauns, "we'll be ready."

Liam and Brendan nodded.

The friends gazed up at the sky. They hoped to see some approaching clouds, but there weren't any. The sky was blue and clear right to the horizon.

Suddenly, Brendan jumped up and started leaping about waving a stick.

"What's wrong?" cried Liam. "Have you been stung by a wasp?"

"No, I'm doing a rain dance to bring some clouds and make it pour," Brendan called.

His trousers fell down again and the leprechaun's chubby face blushed redder than a rose.

"Oops!" Brendan dragged up his trousers and tied his belt in a triple knot. "When we do find a pot of gold, I'll be sure to buy a new belt!"

The friends laughed and laughed.

Going Backwards
To Go Forwards

A thunderstorm woke Liam in the early hours of the morning. Perhaps Brendan danced a little too much, he's not only brought the rain but a storm too.

"What rotten luck!" he grumbled. "It's far too dark to see a rainbow!"

The storm went on and it was still raining at dawn. Liam phoned Chas and then Brendan.

"Get over to mine as soon as you can," he said urgently. "I have a strong feeling it's time to go!"

Liam went out into the pouring rain to check everything was packed on the bus. It had been ready for ages but he wanted to make sure they hadn't forgotten anything.

It wasn't long before a breeze blew the clouds away to reveal the shining sun. Behind a veil of misty rain, a vibrant rainbow appeared in the sky. Liam's hunch was right!

As if by magic, Chas appeared beside him. Liam wouldn't have been surprised if she had clicked her fingers from inside her house and magically transported to his garden. Chas used her hand to shelter her eyes from the bright sun while looking up at the glorious rainbow.

"I can't see where it ends, can you?" she said.

"Somewhere up there," Brendan answered walking towards them and pointing to the north, "but I can't quite see the end either."

"I'll get my binoculars," said Liam.

Liam looked through the glasses and whistled in amazement.

"What is it?" the others asked.

"The rainbow ends at the top of Crooked-Stick Mountain!" he said.

"Then what are we waiting for?" whooped Chas.

"I'll tell Yasmin and Malcolm," said Brendan.

"Yes, good job we sorted the mission statement last week and they both know exactly what we're doing," added Liam.

The three friends found Malcolm the goblin sitting on the wall outside his house.

"He's reading a book," whispered Chas.

"He's always reading a book," Brendan told her. "He's very clever and knows loads of stuff. They say he's the brainiest goblin in the land."

"That's why he'll lead us to the gold," said Liam, jumping down from the bus. "Morning, Malcolm! Ready to go?"

Malcolm looked up from his book.

"Almost, I just need to finish reading this page."

Yasmin was a pixie who was mad about sport. They found her doing some exercises as she waited to be picked up.

"Hi, all," she puffed, "Just two more star jumps to go, be with you in a wiggle of a pixie's ears. Nine, ten! Right, let's go!" she cried, leaping up and into her seat like there were springs on the bottom of her shoes.

Liam drove the bus down a straight road towards rainbow's end. The road wasn't very bumpy so they couldn't sing their bumpy bus song and when Yasmin suggested a pixie song Malcolm grunted his disapproval. He didn't want to be disturbed while reading. Thankfully, It wasn't long before Crooked-Stick Mountain appeared in the distance.

"I hope the pot of gold isn't right at the top," said Brendan, already looking tired before he'd set foot on the mountain.

"That won't be a problem," Yasmin said, grinning broadly. "We can just run up and get it."

"Maybe you can run up a mountain, but I can't."

"Why not?"

"Um ... allergies."

"Don't tell fibs," Liam shouted back from the driver's seat. "Have you never heard the term 'Lazy as a leprechaun', Yasmin?"

"Well, I have now." murmured Yasmin. "Hmm, we'll have to change that to 'lively as a leprechaun'!"

"Not exercise." Groaned Brendan.

At last the bus reached the mountain. Everyone piled out and stood looking up at it. The sun came out from behind a cloud and a flash of light twinkled from the pot of gold at the top of the towering great rock.

"There it is!" yelled Liam.

"Listen up, everyone," Yasmin said in a business-like fashion, "Liam said some elves on motorbikes took off with the last pot of gold you found, that's not going to happen now I'm here. We need to get up that mountainside as fast as we possibly can."

"Can't you just go?" sighed Brendan.

"I won't be able to carry that big heavy pot on my own!" Yasmin retorted.

"She's right, Brendan," said Liam. "Don't be such a lazybones. Let's get on with it."

"Shouldn't bother if I were you," murmured Malcolm. "You won't get very far."

"Why do you say that?" Asked Yasmin, annoyed at being challenged.

He pointed at the trees and bushes between them and the mountain.

"You'll never get through the ancient forest."

"You should be more positive, Malcolm, you won't get anywhere with that attitude!" called Yasmin as she led the charge into the forest. She didn't get far. The path was knotted with tree roots and she tripped over one, falling flat on her face in some nettles. "OUCH!"

Liam couldn't keep up with Yasmin and found himself wandering deeper and deeper into the forest with no sign of the others.

"Where is everyone?" he called out.

Then he turned a corner and fell down a deep hole full of icy water.

"ARRGH! That's C–C–COLD!" he howled.

Meanwhile, Chas and Brendan were running together down a third track. They didn't get far either. Chas slipped on some mud and landed with a painful bump on the ground.

"Bad luck, Chas," called Brendan, from over his shoulder. "Honestly, you're so clumsy."

He ran straight into a wall of rock in front of him, bounced off and his back slammed into the hard ground.

One by one they staggered out of the forest, dirty, battered and bruised.

"Can we get on with the task at hand now that you've all finished mucking about?" said Malcolm, taking a small roll of parchment out of his pocket and marching off. "Follow me. Time is of the essence, remember."

The goblin led the others down to road they had travelled on the bus.

"This can't be right! We're going backwards," called Liam.

"Trust me," said Malcolm.

"And that's not our map you're using," Chas put in. "Sure you know where you're going?"

"Trust me," said Malcolm again.

Muttering and grumbling like children on a boring school outing, they followed their new leader along the road that led away from the mountain.

"Almost there," he called back at last.

"Almost where?" growled Yasmin. "Miles from the gold, you mean!"

"And he says we should trust him," scoffed Brendan, casting his eyes up at the sky.

Liam and his friends were about to give up and go back to the bus when Malcolm led them off the road to a small circle of rocks.

"Take a seat, everyone. Shan't be much longer," he said, holding his ancient map in one hand and bending down to brush some dirt off the ground with the other.

Malcolm took hold of a heavy iron ring in the ground. Straining with all his might, he tugged the ring until a big wooden trapdoor in the ground lifted up and flipped over with a crash that made everyone jump.

"What's down there?" asked Liam, hurrying over and pointing at some stone steps leading into the darkness.

"A secret passageway that leads under the forest and up to mountain top," said Malcolm. "You see, my friends, sometimes you have to go backwards to go forwards."

The other four felt guilty for not believing the strange old goblin and said they were sorry.

"Apology accepted," he said with a smile.

Then he led the way to the underground tunnel. Everyone felt excited about going down it except Brendan.

"I'm scared of the dark," he whispered, shaking like a leaf.

"Here," Yasmin held out her hand, "hold onto me."

Brendan took Yasmin's hand and smiled, glad that the darkness would hide his blushing face.

With Malcolm leading the way and Brendan bringing up the rear, they set off along the tunnel. It was far too dark and with the other's agreement, Chas did a firefly spell and five little glowing bugs appeared in the tunnel to light their way. It was the first time a spell had not backfired and Liam explained that although magic can't solve problems, it can help when magic folk work together in harmony. Navigating the tunnel wasn't too tricky, being beneath the forest they only had to avoid a few deep tree roots. But then they reached the foot of mountain and there was a flight of steep steps going up and up as far as they could see.

"Take your time climbing these stairs, they're quite steep," Malcolm said.

"Yeah right!" said Yasmin, bounding up them. "This is a great way to keep fit!"

Panting and gasping, their legs throbbing and backs aching, the group squeezed through the tiny trapdoor at the top of the tunnel and into the icy air of the mountain.

"If this is what exercise does for you, I'm never doing any more!" wheezed Brendan.

They huddled together, recovering their strength, when a loud rumbling noise rumbled above.

"Look out!" Yasmin screamed, pointing skyward.

A giant snowball was rolling down the mountain towards them, growing bigger and bigger as it went.

"RUN!" yelled Chas.

It was too late! WHUMP! WHUMP! WHUMP! WHUMP! The snowball engulfed Yasmin, Malcolm, Chas and Brendan, carrying them head over heels down the mountainside. Liam had managed to jump out of the way.

"Missed one!" said a deep growly voice. "Let's see you get away from this!"

Looking up, Liam saw a creature with white fur patting some snow together in its hairy paws . There was only one thing it could be.

"Are you a yeti?" asked Liam bravely.

"No, I'm a not-yeti," it growled back.

"A what?"

"A not-yeti. I'm a baby yeti, not yet fully grown."

"What's your name?"

"Not-Yeti!"

"Hello, Not-Yeti," said Liam, holding out his trembling hand. "Pleased to meet you."

Liam had always found the best way to deal with scary situations is to be friendly. It worked well here. Not-Yeti marched over and shook hands, almost yanking Liam's arm out of its socket.

"Don't normally get little magic folk up on my mountain, what do you want?" it asked.

Liam pointed to the pot of gold behind them on the summit.

"We've come to get that," he explained.

"You want that horrible thing?" Not-Yeti chortled. "I like to sleep on that flat bit at the top and that stupid pot is in my way!"

Further down the mountain, Liam's friends had scrambled out of the snowball and brushed the freezing snow from their clothes. Now they were making their way back up, worried sick about what might have happened to their leprechaun friend.

"There he is!" shouted Yasmin.

"A monster's got him! Looks like he's going to throw Liam off the top of the mountain," gasped Brendan.

The others gasped too.

"No, wait!" Malcolm shouted, "They've lifted up the pot of gold and are carrying it down."

"No way!" Yasmin said in shock.

"Yes way, Yasmin, look." Chas pointed, "They've got the gold. HURRAY!"

Together they watched the heavy treasure being carried from the summit by Liam and a furry monster. When the two unlikely pals arrived, Liam introduced his friends to Not-Yeti and they were delighted the creature was friendly.

"How can we ever thank you?" asked Chas.

"Well, there is one thing you could do, I find it hard to sleep with all this flying around up here" it said, indicating to all the litter and plastic bags that had blown up from the human world.

Everyone helped to clear up the rubbish. Then they said goodbye to Not-Yeti and carried the pot of gold over to the tunnel. That's when they realised they had a problem.

"The pot's too big to go through the trapdoor," said Malcolm.

The others looked at each other in horror and all started talking at once...

"We can't carry it down the mountain. There are cliffs and ravines everywhere."

"Not to mention that awful forest at the bottom."

"We'll just have to leave it here."

"What? We can't do that. Not after all we've been through!"

And so it continued until Chas suddenly clapped her hands for silence. She waited a while, grinning, and then pointed to the plastic bags they had just cleared up.

"If we put the gold in these, we can easily carry it down the tunnel," she said.

Everyone cheered this clever idea, including Not-Yeti, who decided to use the empty pot to put any more rubbish in that might find its way up the mountain. Chas was happy everyone liked her suggestion, she smiled and her face shone as brightly as the gold.

Some of the bags split when the gold was put into them, but there was plenty more. They used two or three together to make them strong. Carrying two bags each, they made their way down the steps and along the passage under the forest until they saw a chink of light appear at the other end.

"We've made it!" cheered Yasmin.

"Don't speak too soon," warned Brendan. "There might be robber elves waiting to steal our treasure."

However, there was nothing outside but the singing of the birds and the whistling of the chilly north wind. They marched back along the road and collapsed onto the bus with groans of exhaustion and sighs of relief.

"Time to go home," said Liam.

On the way, they remembered to stop and give some of the gold to Albert and Violet. Then Yasmin and Malcolm were dropped off at their homes and the three friends drove back to Liam's house with their share of the treasure. It was late when they got in and they all crashed out for the night. Next morning, feeling much better, they sat outside in the garden to have breakfast. Suddenly, Chas's face fell and she started to cry.

"Whatever's the matter?" asked Liam.

"I don't want our adventure to be over," sobbed Chas. "It was really hard at times, but I've enjoyed every minute of it."

"We found the gold in the end," said Brendan, patting her on the back.

"That's right," Liam agreed, "but it's not the most important thing. It's what we learned. Now we know a trip has to be carefully planned, everyone has to have the same thing in mind and you should never be afraid to take a backwards step if it helps to achieve your aim."

"There's one other thing, Liam," added Chas, reaching out and holding the leprechaun's hands. "We've learned the value of friendship. That's more precious than all the treasure in the world."

A few days later, when some of the gold had been used to buy the things they needed, Liam held a party for everyone who'd been on their epic journeys with them and all their neighbours from Leprechaun Lane. Their friends arrived wearing smart new clothes and the neighbours joined them tucking into the spread of party food, of which only the dishes Violet brought went untouched, well, except for Albert who ate a huge bowl of gobblegum porridge.

It was a very happy occasion and the neighbours were soon asking Liam if they too could go on a quest to find a pot of gold.

Liam told them that helping others was now his new job. Like his grandfather before him, he was going to be a treasure hunter and bring gold back for everyone.

They all cheered for Liam. Then danced and laughed and sang late into the evening. Brendan couldn't help doing a little jig and when his trousers didn't fall down, like they usually did, he pulled up his waistcoat to reveal a shiny gold buckle.

"New belt!" He shouted with glee.

Laughter erupted and the party continued with lots of excited chatter about Liam's next big adventure.

The End

About the Author

Andy Donnell recently took early retirement from his job as a CEO in the field of Facility Management and decided to write Get On My Bus as a children's story that demonstrated effective teamwork, planning and business management strategy. If you don't know what Facility Management is, then let me explain...

When you visit an airport, a hotel, a factory, or anywhere where there are lots of people working together, there is someone making sure that everyone who goes in and out of that building, whether they're working or visiting, can go about their business to the best of their ability and without having to worry about a thing.

Making sure there are enough cups at the water dispenser, that the bins are emptied, that the staff are fully trained in case of an emergency, that the building is safe and that everyone feels heard, that's the role of someone who works in facility management. Beavering away in the background, making sure that everything is in its right place at the right time and everyone knows what their job is, the facility manager looks at the big picture and finds solutions to make each tiny part work as a whole. When each aspect goes to plan, businesses run optimally, people are happier, and the jobs that need to be done get done well. Pretty cool, yeah?

When Andy retired he decided to share his knowledge of business planning and management to encourage young people to grow their own businesses. But businesses aren't just about the pot of gold at the end of the rainbow, like in Liam's story, they are about people - like Chas, Brendan and Malcolm, and plans. When we work together as a team and plan our journey, we can get where we want to be.

Andy now mentors entrepreneurs through The Prince's Trust and also volunteers his time with charities that help people through difficult times in their lives, so they too can find their path. He believes that with the right support and structure, anyone can achieve their dream. And what better time to sow the seeds of those dreams than childhood?

Dream big and work hard,
then maybe you can find your pot of gold.

More titles from
A Spark in the Sand

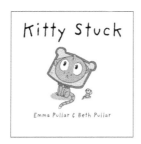

£7.99
ISBN 978-1-9998240-4-4
Kitty Stuck
Emma Pullar and Beth Pullar
Kitty is a calamitous cat who finds himself in some rather sticky situations. Fortunately, his loving family are always close on hand to help him get unstuck.

£7.99
ISBN 978-1-9998240-0-6
Peter Digs a Den
Amy Stretch-Parker and Kate Brunskill
Peter is a small boy with a big dream; to dig a den big enough for his entire family and all their pets to sleep in. But first he needs the right tool.

Titles available to buy online at
www.asparkinthesand.co.uk

Lightning Source UK Ltd.
Milton Keynes UK
UKHW02f2236101018
330344UK00013B/1586/P